3 4143 10159 6946

Finn M[acCool] the Giant's Causeway

An Irish Folk Tale

written by Charlotte Guillain ☀ illustrated by Steve Dorado

Raintree

Raintree is an imprint of Capstone Global Library Limited, a company incorporated in England and Wales having its registered office at 7 Pilgrim Street, London, EC4V 6LB – Registered company number: 6695582

www.raintree.co.uk
myorders@raintree.co.uk

Edited by Daniel Nunn, Rebecca Rissman, Sian Smith, and Gina Kammer
Designed by Joanna Hinton-Malivoire and Peggie Carley
Original illustrations © Capstone Global Library Ltd 2014
Illustrated by Steve Dorado
Production by Victoria Fitzgerald
Originated by Capstone Global Library Ltd
Printed and bound in China by RR Donnelley Asia

ISBN 978 1 406 28133 0 (paperback)
18 17 16 15 14
10 9 8 7 6 5 4 3 2 1

ISBN 978 1 406 28140 8 (big book)
18 17 16 15 14
10 9 8 7 6 5 4 3 2 1

British Library Cataloguing in Publication Data
A full catalogue record for this book is available from the British Library.

Characters

Finn MacCool,
an Irish giant

Finn's wife, Saba

Red Man, a
Scottish giant

There was once an Irish giant called Finn MacCool.

He liked to fight the giants who lived in Scotland, so he built a pathway across the sea, called a causeway, from Ireland to Scotland.

One day, Finn told a Scottish giant called Red Man to come and fight him. When Red Man started to cross the pathway, Finn realized the Scottish giant was much bigger than he was! He ran away home to hide.

When Finn got home, he jumped into the bathtub, and his wife, Saba, threw a blanket over him. Then there was a very loud knock at the door.

When Saba opened the door,
Red Man boomed, "Where is
Finn? I want to fight him!"

Saba replied, "Finn is out hunting, but you are welcome to come inside and wait."

Saba pointed to a huge log
leaning against the wall of the
house. "You are welcome to leave
your spear next to Finn's," she
told Red Man.

Then Saba baked some bread
for Red Man, hiding a saucepan
in the middle. When Red Man bit
into the pan, he broke his teeth.
Saba smiled and said, "This is
the bread that Finn likes best!"

Next Saba gave Red Man a
bucket full of ale. "This is Finn's
favourite mug," she said.

"He must be very big,"
said Red Man nervously.

Then Saba told Red Man that she needed to feed the baby. She threw some bread to Finn in the bathtub, and he moved under the blanket. Red Man thought Finn was the baby!

Red Man ran from the house, crying, "If the baby is that big, then how big is his father?"

He ran all the way back to Scotland across the pathway.

Finn jumped out of the bathtub
and chased Red Man, throwing
rocks after him. He smashed up
the pathway he had built so that
only the jagged ends near the
shorelines were left.

The end

The moral of the story

Many traditional stories have a moral. This is a lesson you can learn from the story. The moral of this story is that we should always think before acting. Finn challenged Red Man to a fight without finding out how big he was first! This story also teaches us that very often brains can beat strength.

The origins of *Finn MacCool and the Giant's Causeway*

Nobody knows who first told the story of *Finn MacCool and the Giant's Causeway*, but the story comes from Ireland. There are many Irish stories about this character. This story is supposed to tell us how the Giant's Causeway was made. The Giant's Causeway is a rock formation in the sea between Ireland and Scotland that was really caused by a volcano erupting. People used to tell stories like this for entertainment before we had television, radio, or computers. The story has been passed on by Irish storytellers over hundreds of years, with different storytellers making their own changes to it over time. Eventually, people began to write the story down, and so it has spread around the world.